LISA
OVERLAND TO
CARIBOO
PRISCILLA GALLOWAY

LISA
OVERLAND TO
CARIBOO

PRISCILLA GALLOWAY

PENGUIN
CANADA

PENGUIN CANADA

Published by the Penguin Group

Penguin Books, a division of Pearson Canada, 10 Alcorn Avenue, Toronto, Ontario, Canada M4V 3B2

Penguin Books Ltd, 80 Strand, London WC2R 0RL, England

Penguin Putnam Inc., 375 Hudson Street, New York, New York 10014, U.S.A.

Penguin Books Australia Ltd, 250 Camberwell Road, Camberwell, Victoria 3124, Australia

Penguin Books India (P) Ltd, 11, Community Centre, Panchsheel Park, New Delhi – 110 017, India

Penguin Books (NZ) Ltd, cnr Rosedale and Airborne Roads, Albany, Auckland 1310, New Zealand

Penguin Books (South Africa) (Pty) Ltd, 24 Sturdee Avenue, Rosebank 2196, South Africa

Penguin Books Ltd, Registered Offices: 80 Strand, London WC2R 0RL, England

FIRST PUBLISHED 2003

1 3 5 7 9 10 8 6 4 2

COPYRIGHT © PRISCILLA GALLOWAY, 2003

ILLUSTRATIONS © SHARON MATTHEWS, 2003

DESIGN: MATTHEWS COMMUNICATIONS DESIGN INC.

MANUFACTURED IN CANADA.

NATIONAL LIBRARY OF CANADA CATALOGUING IN PUBLICATION

Galloway, Priscilla, 1930-
Lisa, book 1 : overland to Cariboo / Priscilla Galloway.
(Our Canadian girl)
For ages 8–12.
ISBN 0-14-100327-8

1. Cariboo Region (B.C.)—Gold discoveries—Juvenile fiction.
I. Title. II. Title: Overland to Cariboo. III. Title: Lisa, book one.
IV. Series.

PS8563.A45L58 2003   jC813'.54   C2003-903870-7
PZ7

Visit Penguin Books' website at **www.penguin.ca**

In memory of
Margaret Peebles McNaughton and
Catherine O'Hare Schubert,
brave girls and remarkable women in
Canada's history,
and of Joan (Brownie) Peebles,
my operatic aunt,
whose memories of her own Aunt Margaret
inspired me

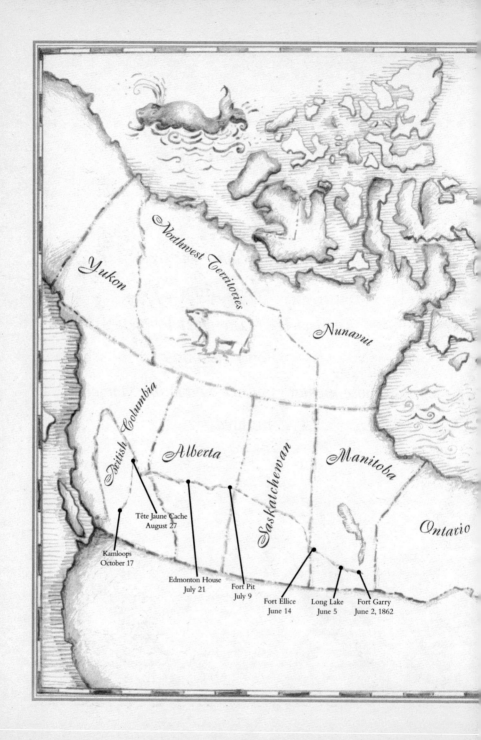

Yukon

Northwest Territories

Nunavut

British Columbia

Alberta

Saskatchewan

Manitoba

Ontario

Tête Jaune Cache
August 27

Kamloops
October 17

Edmonton House
July 21

Fort Pit
July 9

Fort Ellice
June 14

Long Lake
June 5

Fort Garry
June 2, 1862

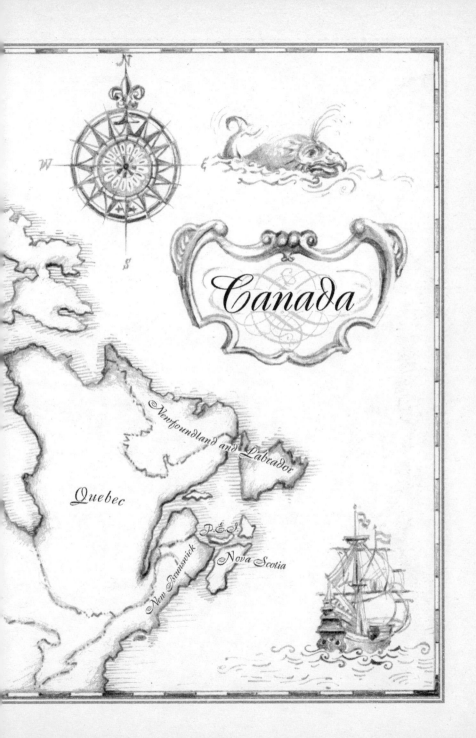

INTRODUCTION

IN 1858, PROSPECTORS DISCOVERED GOLD ALONG THE Fraser River in British Columbia. More than 30,000 gold-seekers journeyed north to the goldfields that year. Most of them were unsuccessful and disappointed, and many gave up and went back home again. Others, however, continued to work their way up the river, still looking for gold, and they found it, early in 1862, on Williams Creek in the Cariboo.

In the spring of that year, one hundred and fifty men, mostly young and single, set out from "Canada" (present-day Quebec and Ontario) to journey overland to the Cariboo goldfields. Other men, eager to strike it rich, joined them along the way, swelling the number of the determined "Overlanders" to two hundred.

It was an amazing journey: five months, mostly on foot, across the Prairies, through bogs and marshes, across one of the highest mountain ranges in the world, and down a river teeming with violent rapids. Death stalked the travellers in many forms: starvation, being kicked by a horse or crushed under the wheels of an ox-drawn cart, drowning while crossing a river, or being dashed on the rocks when a raft was wrecked.

At the town of Fort Garry, now Winnipeg, one brave family became part of the expedition: Augustus Schubert, his wife, Catherine, and their three young children. Both Augustus and Catherine were recent immigrants to Canada, he from Germany and she from Ireland. Though many of the men must have thought it impossible for a woman and children to survive the hardships of the long journey—little food, endless walking, blazing sun and terrible storms, little medical care—the Schubert family would prove them wrong.

For this story, I have imagined that the Schubert family had a ten-year-old niece, Lisa. Unlike the other characters in this story, Lisa did not actually exist, but I'm sure all the Schuberts often wished she did.

My great-aunt Margaret Peebles married Archibald McNaughton, one of the Overlanders, in 1890. She compiled a book about the journey, based on recollections and on written records, and it was published in 1896 with the title *Overland to Cariboo: an Eventful*

Journey of Canadian Pioneers to the Gold-Fields of British Columbia in 1862. In it she wrote:

> Mrs. Schubert passed through all the experiences of this long journey, and showed the most remarkable endurance and energy. She had the care of three young children, and in all the dangers and disasters which the party underwent, she and her children came through safe and sound. The day following their arrival at Kamloops, Mrs. Schubert gave birth to a daughter ...

For a ten-year-old girl like Lisa, the journey would mean physical hardships, demanding work, grown-up responsibilities—and the adventure of a lifetime!

CHAPTER 1

"*Don't leave me behind, Papa. I'll run* after you, and that's a promise." *I won't cry*, I told myself fiercely, but I could feel the tears on my face. My nose always itched when I cried. I sneezed again and again.

"*Gesundheit.*" Papa patted my head. "Liesl," he said, "you can't come. Your ma needs you here in Fort Garry."

Papa (Uncle Augustus, really) was always more patient with me than with his own three children. I loved him very much, and I did try

1

not to provoke him, though Ma would say it didn't always look that way. Sometimes the words just burst out.

"She's not my real ma," I said, "and you're not my real papa. They're dead. And my name's not Liesl, I'm Lisa now."

"Good for you, girl," said Ma. Hands on her hips, she glared at Papa, her black eyes flashing.

"Ma, aren't you angry at me?" I stammered.

"I will be, if you forget your manners one more time. Right now, I have other things on my mind. Like telling this man I married we're not staying in Fort Garry without him. We've talked enough these past few weeks, Augustus. If you are going off gold mining in the Cariboo, we are going too, and that's the way of it. Dry your face, Lisa. Chin up, girl. You hear me, husband? What do you have to say?"

"Are you setting yourself against me, woman?"

"Would I do such a thing? It's just that sometimes I know you better than you know yourself, and this is one of those times."

Papa took off his glasses and wiped them with his white handkerchief. "One stubborn female in a family oughtta be enough," he grumbled. "How come I got two of them? I'll worry if I leave you behind; I'll worry if I take you. Dunno which is worse." He settled his glasses on his broad nose and made a face at Ma and me. Then he grinned. "Can't say I wouldn't rather have my family along," he added. "It will be hard, though, going to Cariboo."

I cleared my throat. "I've made hard trips already." My real mama died on the ship coming to America when I was born. Pa raised me in Boston till he took sick, then we went to Uncle Augustus out west in St. Paul. We got there just in time for Pa to die. That was the first hard journey that I remember. Uncle Augustus and Aunt Catherine took me in. I slipped into calling them Ma and Papa, like one of their own. That's mostly how I felt, in spite of what I'd just said.

"You think it'll be easier than when we came to Fort Garry?" Papa asked. "Far as I recall, you were cold and scared all the way."

From St. Paul to Fort Garry, that was my second hard journey. Far as *I* recalled, we were *all* cold and scared. I wasn't the only one.

We'd never have left St. Paul, except for the Indians. When settlers came into the Sioux lands, they chased the Natives out. Then—Papa told me—the government didn't pay what they'd promised in their treaty. The Sioux were hungry and miserable. No wonder they were angry at folks like us.

I knew enough to be extra careful around the Sioux who came into St. Paul to trade, because they liked yellow hair like mine so much. Over the years, more than one blond child had been snatched away into captivity. We hadn't begun worrying about Jamie, though. He was a tiny baby without much hair, just fuzz, as light and soft as cornsilk.

Those Indians surely must have sharp eyes! One night, a Sioux brave broke into our house. He smashed the back window and grabbed the baby out of his cradle. Lucky thing I was there! I screamed. Ma was serving beer in the big front room, but Papa came running with the poker. The Indian dropped Jamie, but Papa chased after him and beat him up. I told Papa that the Indian was a coward, not a brave, trying to steal a baby.

Next night, forty Sioux came looking for Papa. The leaders beat on the door, but it held. They began coming round every few days after that. The Sioux are warriors, and Papa had beaten one of them. We knew they would not forget. We all stayed in the house and barred the door. If Papa had to go out for supplies, two other men followed him with their rifles handy. Ma was terrified for Jamie and me, but she knew that the other children weren't safe either. If the Sioux captured one of us, they would take us far away.

Our business was ruined. Who would come to a tavern where the door was always barred? After a couple of weeks, we sold the stock, packed up, and left in the dark. We kept looking back, but we were lucky; no trackers followed us. Perhaps the Sioux were getting ready for winter. It was cold when we set out, and turned colder as we went north.

"It was October when we came to Fort Garry," I reminded Papa. "It's June now. Summer is the best time to travel."

"It could be October when we get to the Cariboo," said Papa.

"Nonsense," Ma broke in. "August, most likely. I don't like Fort Garry, Augustus. I don't like the floods. And how am I supposed to run a tavern and a farm by myself, and look after the children as well? If we were getting rich, it might be different, but we're only scraping by. And what if there's more trouble here, like there was in St. Paul? We should go with you; Lisa's right."

"Is she? The Overlanders will ride fast and hard. They left their own wives and children back east. Maybe they won't *let* us travel with them."

Before Ma could reply, Pierre came in with a pail of water, his brother Alain at his heels. Pierre and Alain worked for us on the farm. They had come from Montreal.

"All of you going to Cariboo, *n'est-ce pas*, boss?" Pierre asked. "Take us too, eh? We work hard."

"Is this a plot? Did my wife talk to you?" Papa frowned, but not as if he were really angry. Then he chuckled. "*Certainement*, boys, we're all going, you too. Tell you the truth, Pierre, I'm not sorry." He slapped Pierre on the back. "One man with his wife and children, that's not so good. Three men will be much better."

"That's settled then," said Ma. "The Overlanders plan to leave tomorrow. Mr. Morrow's party ordered breakfast at sunup. But we can't be ready that fast, can we?"

"We'll not be far behind them," said Papa. "They're new to this; they won't move fast. Until their feet are toughened, most of them will be nursing blisters."

"We're tough, aren't we," Gus boasted.

"We're not tenderfeet," Papa agreed. "The Bishop recommended Charles Rochette, and he's been hired as guide. I hope he's as good as the

Bishop thinks. Now listen to me, all of you—Gus and Lisa, you especially; this is serious. Don't tell anyone that you and Ma are going. It mustn't get back to the Overlanders. We'll catch up, but not for a few days, when it's too late for them to send us back. They won't make us travel alone."

"They'll teach me to pan for gold," I announced, nearly bursting with excitement. "I asked Mr. McNaughton and he said he would if I was there. He made me a promise, and he said a McNaughton never goes back on his word." I twirled around on my toes. Ma made a face at me. She always wanted me to do girl things, like laundry and cooking.

"He never expected to keep that promise." Ma sounded angry. "Gold panning, indeed! He deceived you, Lisa. He never expected to see you again."

"They should teach *me*," little Gus chimed in. "I'm a boy." Gus hated to be left out, but sometimes Papa said he was getting too big for his britches.

"Keep out of the Overlanders' way, both of you," said Papa sharply. "Mind what I say." He tugged on his beard, thinking. "We'll be eight souls," he said. "Our wagon won't be big enough. We'll need a Red River cart as well, and oxen. I've bought the mining gear already, but we'll need a second tent."

Mining gear! I could almost see the glint of gold.

Papa teased, "Now that we're closing the tavern, I'd best trade the rest of the whiskey. Maybe that will make my little Irish wife happy."

Ma hated the liquor business, and Papa knew it. She would say whiskey was the devil's own drink, and it was a sorry sight to watch the men throwing their money away when their wives and children needed them at home—and it didn't make her any happier that they threw their money away in our tavern. Now she sniffed. "You'll not be fooling me, Augustus. If the kegs were lighter, I know you'd be taking the whiskey with us, no matter if I was happy or not."

She glared at Papa, then her face softened. Her dark eyes gleamed. Ma never can stay mad for more than five minutes, especially when she's got what she wanted. She dug in her pocket and pulled out a list. "We must have pemmican."

"I hate pemmican," Gus whined.

I don't like pemmican myself, I thought, *but I'd eat it, grease and all, if there was nothing else.*

"Lisa and I will pack," said Ma. "Gus, take Mary Jane out to play, but don't wander off. Lisa, we'll start with the crockery."

We worked quietly for a few minutes, then Ma put her hand on my arm. "Lisa," she began, then stopped. She looked—strangely—shy.

"What is it?"

"Since you came to our family, you've been Papa's girl, Lisa," she said at last (as if I needed telling!), "but on this journey, I shall need you more than he will. I wish you were older. Sometimes I will be tired. Then you must look out for the young ones and help with the food and washing; you must be another woman in this family."

Ma, tired? Ma was never tired. And I wanted to be a miner, not "another woman in the family." But Ma was talking as if I was grown up already, as if she could depend on me. I liked that.

"I'll help lots, Ma," I promised.

CHAPTER N.º 2

On Monday morning, Papa traded our smart carriage and some whiskey for a two-wheeled Red River cart and three oxen—one to pull the cart, one for our wagon, and the third to spell off the other two.

"I kept the pony team," Papa said. "Sometimes we'll need two, or maybe all three oxen to pull the wagon. Then we'll be glad to have horses to pull the cart."

"You kept the milk cows?" Ma asked sharply.

"Of course, Catherine. I know you and the

children will need fresh milk."

"You didn't trade Star, did you?" I asked him. Star was Ma's own riding horse. He was black as coal, except for the white blaze on his face. When he nibbled a carrot off my hand, his nose felt as soft as baby Jamie's cheeks.

"Would I trade your ma's horse? Of course not." Papa's big hand patted my head.

Gus clambered up into the cart and grabbed the reins. The ox just stood there, even when he called "Giddup."

Papa laughed and lifted him down. "Off you go and help your ma," he said.

"Can I drive the cart?" I asked.

"You can lead the spare ox," said Papa. "The animals don't need more weight to pull."

"Do we have to walk, then? Papa, my boots are too tight."

"We mostly have to walk, Lisa. The little ones don't weigh enough to make a difference, but you do."

"I guess you won't let me drive the wagon, either."

Papa made a face at me. "The wagon will be heavier than the cart. Four hundred pounds of pemmican, seven hundred of flour, water casks, all our gear..." He sighed. "Lisa, I'm afraid there won't be room for your trunk."

"Papa!" My dead mother's dresses were in that old humpbacked trunk, along with Dad's shirts and trousers. I used to bury my face in them and pretend that Dad was away someplace, that he'd come in the door any day, and I'd hug him and never let go. His razor was there, and the belt he used to strop it. Mother's dishes, ready for my own kitchen when I grew up. A little bundle of letters that I could not read because they were written in German; Papa had promised to read them to me one day.

"I'm sorry. You can pack one of your ma's dresses. Say, what about her boots? Wear them. Stuff newspaper in the toes and wear two pairs of socks." Papa smiled. "Dig out those old letters now, Lisa. We'll put them with my papers."

Papa wrapped the papers in two layers of

oilskin, tied with string. "I'll stow them under the seat in the cart. If we're attacked by Indians, or tumbled into a river, if anything happens to me or Ma, you hang on to them."

I shivered. "Yes, Papa."

Papa patted my shoulder. "That's the girl."

"When we hit gold, can we send for my trunk?"

"We can, and our furniture as well, if we still want it. You can have a new trunk, full of fancy clothes, when we hit gold."

CHAPTER N.º 3

My mother's dark-blue diary was the first thing I saw when I opened my trunk. She began it during her voyage to America, before I was born. The first two pages were filled with her cramped writing—in German—but the entries soon tapered off to nothing. Father had told me Mama was too seasick to write any more.

I hugged the little book, even though seeing it again made me cry. Then I thought, *I can use this book for my own diary of our journey to Cariboo.* Papa opened his precious oilskin package to add the slim volume, but he didn't think my diary idea would work. I soon found out he was right. There was no place in our Red River cart to settle with book and pencil, and there were no candles or lamps to spare. Besides, when my evening chores were done, I was bone-tired.

Ma suggested that I should keep a kind of diary in my head, telling myself the story of each day before I fell asleep. "Make a tale for your children," she said. "That's what I did when I left home."

Ma could tell a fine tale, but she was seventeen when she left Ireland. I was only ten. Besides, I didn't expect to have children. Babies meant husbands, and who would want to marry a plum pudding like me? Even if I wanted to, which I did not.

I wanted to be a miner, shaking my pan and finding pieces of gold in the bottom, or breaking up rocks with my pickaxe and finding gold there. I wanted to live in a tent. It would be a hard life, but I knew it would be better than forever cooking and washing and sewing—and wiping Mary

Jane's runny nose and changing Jamie's smelly pants. I'd have to live in Indian country, though. That could be dangerous.

Remembering the Sioux riding up to our house and banging on the door, I put my arms around Ma and hugged her. She hugged back. Ma gave great hugs.

"Have you been off in your dreams, Lisa? Are you worried about our journey?"

"Indians," I muttered. "Will the Sioux attack us? Papa says it's a long way to the Cariboo. What if we get lost?"

"When the journey begins, the traveller does not always know where the road will lead."

When Ma talked like that, all solemn and mystical, I got a shiver down my spine. It was a seldom thing, and just as well. It was discomforting.

"However," Ma went on briskly, "we will not pass through Sioux country, and I do not intend for any of us to get lost."

"I don't either," I said.

That night, like many others later, we lay on buffalo hides spread on the ground. Wrapped in a feather bed, I was warm and comfy, except that my feet were on fire from walking. Ma slept on my left, her dark curls almost lost under the blankets. Papa, beside her, snored gently. Hearing him, I stopped worrying about Indians, or getting lost.

The sky was black velvet. The stars were brilliant points of light. The Milky Way made a path over my head, pointing west. On my right side, Gus and Mary Jane snuggled together. Little Jamie slept beside Ma, and Alain and Pierre were a short distance away. We had planned to put up the tents, but we were too tired. The night was cool, but not cold. In those first weeks, it never rained.

That night, I decided I would milk the cows every morning and night. I was scared of them,

Bossy especially. But the cows were not as big as the oxen, and I wasn't scared of *them*. Bessie would let her milk down nice and easy, but Bossy liked to twitch her tail and try to kick over the milking pail. I just wouldn't let her. Miners had to be brave. So did the women in our family. I could practise being brave by milking the cows.

CHAPTER N° 4

We caught up with the Overlanders at Long Lake on Thursday morning, after three days of slapping at blackflies on the trail. We had tied mitts onto Mary Jane's hands so that she couldn't scratch. I was about ready to tie mitts onto my own hands; every bit of bare skin itched like fire.

At Long Lake, the men were meeting to choose leaders and make rules. There were one hundred and fifty people and one hundred and twenty carts.

Mr. Thomas McMicking was chosen captain, probably because his group of twenty-four men from Queenston was the biggest. We had only seven people from Fort Garry: Papa, Ma, Pierre and Alain, me, Gus, and Mary Jane, not counting baby Jamie. Papa was our leader.

Papa asked Mr. McMicking to leave the meeting for a few minutes to talk with us. "Please accept us as part of your company," he said. "We have experience."

"I hardly think it's fitting," said Mr. McMicking. The way he talked, I thought he must be from Scotland. "Har-r-r-dly" sounded like a whole sentence, not just one disapproving word. I shivered. Would Mr. McMicking turn our family away?

"We travel fast and hard," he continued. "It's gold we're after, man; we canna wait for your goodwife and the wee bairns."

Ma had so far kept quiet, but now she spoke up. "I walked the width of Ireland to take ship for America. All my family died in the famine, except for my brother Kevin, who walked with me, but Kevin died on the ship and was buried at sea. It was a lonely time for me until Mr. Schubert came into my life." Ma's face lighted like a lamp as she glanced at Papa. "After our marriage, we walked and rode across America to St. Paul, a long way farther than across all of Ireland, as you must know, and then from St. Paul to Fort Garry. I'm maybe a bit softer now, Mr. McMicking, but I'll harden fast. I'll not hold you back, nor will my children."

"That's my Catherine!" Papa's eyes shone. "You can depend on her."

"Well," said Mr. McMicking. He was quiet for a long time. "There's this to be said in favour: we shall meet natives on the way. One hundred and fifty men might look like a war party, but when the natives see a woman and children, they will know that we travel in peace. Let me put it to the company."

Some of the men grumbled, but they agreed that we might travel with them. No special treatment, though—and we must not slow their journey. Humph! I saw plenty of men soaking their blisters yesterday. Mr. Morrow and his men were the only Overlanders I knew, because they had taken their meals with us. They had travelled by stagecoach and boat all the way to Fort Garry, even waiting twelve days at Georgetown for the steamship *International* to be finished, so they wouldn't have to ride or walk the last four hundred miles. I figured we were going to keep up just fine.

Ma gave us dinner, our noon meal, and had Papa's ready when he came back from the meeting. He told us the first rule. We would have to get up at three o'clock every morning, before sunrise, to be ready to leave at five. Every single day, except Sunday. I hadn't expected the journey would be *that* hard.

Pierre and Alain harnessed our oxen while Papa ate. Soon the train began to move off under the blazing sun. We fell into place near the end, behind Mr. Morrow and the men from

Montreal, including Mr. McNaughton, who said I'd better call him Archie. Talk about noise! Oxen and horses snorted, mooed, or whinnied, dogs yipped, carts creaked, and men yelled at their beasts and at each other. Even Alain said a bad word, in French. "Gus, Mary Jane, Lisa, you put your hands over your ears," Ma snapped. "If I ever hear you using those words, I'll wash your mouths out with soap."

As soon as we were moving, I climbed up on Star and rode a little way off to look at the whole train. At the front, carts and riders glittered in the sun, but beasts and men kicked up tremendous clouds of dust, which got darker and thicker as my eyes moved along the line; I could hardly see my family. I tasted dust with every breath as I rode back.

"Pull up your bonnet, Lisa," said Ma, as soon as she saw me. "You'll be as brown as an Indian! And don't you go off again without asking me."

I wouldn't have minded being as brown as the Sioux girls, so proud and tall, though I would not have traded my golden curls for their long black braids.

Ma did look tired. Gus had the corner of her apron in his mouth. I slid down off Star. "Sorry, Ma," I said, "I didn't think. Come on, Gus, walk with me."

Papa was driving the wagon. Mary Jane snuggled against him, her head nodding drowsily.

"Do we have to walk in the dust all the time?" I asked. "It's not fair."

"No, we don't," replied Papa. "Mr. McMicking's party is leading today. Tomorrow, those carts will go to the end of the train. Mr. Wattie will lead. We will move forward every day until it's our turn in front, then we'll go to the back and start over. That's fair, isn't it?"

Pierre got seasick the next day. So did some other men, though there wasn't any ocean. The tall prairie grass swayed in the wind like waves. The rest of us from Fort Garry were not sick, and everybody soon got used to the rocking wagons and the swaying grass.

CHAPTER N°. 5

We had a lot to learn. The next day, we passed small lakes and rivers all morning. So when we stopped at noon beside a lake, we dipped water to drink with our dinner, but we did not take time to fill our water casks. Everybody thought we could easily do that when we stopped for the evening. Then, all afternoon, we never came to another stream or lake. Without water, we could not stop at suppertime.

I walked beside Alain. Both my heels had blisters. The breeze had died. I swatted mosquitoes and scratched my itches. At last I heard a croaking noise.

"Bullfrogs?" Bullfrogs meant water.

"Ain't that sweet music," said Ma, "the prettiest sound since Fort Garry." After that, we filled our water casks and canteens every time we could.

Sometimes the water was no good to drink. Some lakes were too salty. And some lakes and streams had dried up, except for little sloughs covered with green scum. We strained the water through a clean shirt into a cooking pot, and Ma boiled it over the fire. It tasted awful, but if we boiled it long enough, we did not get sick.

At night we pulled our carts together to make a big triangle, with the fronts facing out. We pitched our tents and slept outside of the triangle, but we tethered our animals inside it, so nobody could sneak off with them. "This is Blackfoot country," our guide said. "If the Indians raid our camp, they will try to take the horses and oxen. They won't bother with people." In the daytime, I believed him, but at night I was not so sure.

Men took turns watching, two guards on each side. Ma wanted to take a turn, and so did I, but the men laughed at us. Ma said never mind, we could sew on buttons or bake some extra bannock bread.

The cows turned skittish at night, with so many other animals around and no pasture. I milked them as soon as we stopped for supper, before they were penned up.

Near the end of our first week, we camped by a lake as clear as glass. Papa and I went fishing. Archie came too. Papa cut an elm branch for my fishing pole and tied a line on the end. He showed me how to tie my fishhook with a figure-eight knot and made me practise until I could do it to suit him. "We can't afford to lose a fishhook because you tied it wrong," he told me.

That lake was full of fish. I caught three little

trout. They jerked around on the bank until Archie banged them on the head.

"Will I clean them for you, or will you do it yourself?" he asked.

"I guess miners clean their own fish," I said.

"They do," Archie agreed.

"I'm going to be a miner, so I'll do it, if you'll show me how."

Archie looked at his big knife. "Suppose I cut them open and you do the rest."

With Archie beside me, it was easy to pull out their insides and wash my fish in the lake. Papa caught more trout, and we cleaned them too. We had plenty for dinner and breakfast. Archie skewered mine and showed me how to roast them over the hot coals. I felt sorry for the trout when I caught them, but they were mighty good to eat. I gave Ma my biggest fish, and she picked every morsel off the bones.

"I guess you can't clean fish, Ma," I boasted. Papa had always cleaned the fish he caught.

"I can if I have to," Ma admitted. "It's not too

different from cleaning chickens. I'm likely not as good as you, though. You are helping me a lot, Lisa, just as I hoped."

I still felt warm and happy when I fell asleep that night.

On our second Saturday we came to the riverbank across from Fort Ellice. We could see a wall of poles and some houses. People came down and waved. The Hudson's Bay Company kept a flat boat on the river, but it was only big enough for one cart and one ox, and we had more than a hundred carts! It was late afternoon before the last one crossed. Fort Ellice was dirty, and the buildings were falling down, but we camped there anyway. Mr. McKay, the factor, welcomed us.

Archie got out his tin whistle. Papa unpacked his fiddle. Everywhere in camp, people got together to sing and play. Nobody went to bed early that night, and nobody cared. The next day would be the Sabbath, the one morning we did not have to get up in the dark.

Sunday dawned cold and windy. Rain beat against our tents. Mr. McMicking had read the Bible and led us in prayer the week before. I liked it better than regular church in St. Paul. At Fort Ellice, Mr. McKay invited us to his house, where a visiting minister was going to preach at 1:00 p.m. On the bright side, we were able to stay dry. However, we were all squashed together, and the sermon was more than two hours long!

It was still raining next morning. We were not used to packing up in the rain, though we would soon learn. We waited until early afternoon, hoping the rain would stop. It didn't.

We left Fort Ellice after dinner. Soon we came to a steep hill that led down to another river. Our carts were near the end of the train that day, and the hill was one big mudslide when our turn came. Papa waited at the top. On the slope ahead, Mr. Morrow's ox slipped and slithered in the mud. Suddenly it began to run. I could see Mr. Morrow's hat behind the ox, and Archie, behind the cart, trying to set the brake. Then the hat disappeared, and somebody screamed. Ma turned white.

"Stay here, all of you," Papa ordered. He took off his glasses and gave them to me, then he too began to slide down the hill, churning up more mud as he went.

Soon Papa and Archie carried a limp body down to the river. We were sure Mr. Morrow had been killed. The wheel of the cart had gone right over his head. Dr. Stevenson tended to him, though, and he did not die. The mud was so soft that his head had been pressed into it, and he was saved.

*On the slope ahead, Mr.
Morrow's ox slipped and
slithered in the mud.*

After the accident, lots of men came to help our cart and all the others get down to the river safely. There were no more runaways.

The scow that worked this river was big enough for two carts, so we crossed faster than at Fort Ellice, but the Hudson's Bay Company charged fifty cents a cart, sixty dollars for all of us. Archie and I thought it was too much money.

We put up our tents in the rain. All our bedding was wet. That was the first time we had to lie down in wet clothes. I was cold all night, and Jamie coughed. The sun came out the next day, though, lovely and hot. We spread our tents and bedding to dry when we stopped for dinner. Mr. McMicking gave us an extra hour, but we kept going for an extra hour before supper, to make up the time.

"Papa," I said, "when we get to the Cariboo, can we build a house before we start finding gold?"

"Let's get to the Cariboo first," Papa said.

CHAPTER N.º 7

We picked our first strawberries at the end of June. Then on July 4, in a river valley, we came to fields of green plants and gleaming red berries, the biggest I had ever seen. Ma tied our Red River cart behind the wagon. Papa drove, and Pierre tied the riding horses behind him. Alain drove the other animals. The rest of us picked strawberries, even Mary Jane, until she got too far behind and I had to run back for her and hand her up to Papa and Jamie.

I picked my apron full, and so did Ma. Even

Gus picked as many berries as he ate. Bossy did not try any nonsense when I milked her; she knew I would not put up with it. Supper that evening was strawberries and cream, all we could eat. Ma always traded our extra milk or cream, or sold it. Men lined up for it that day.

After we left Fort Ellice, it was a long way to Carleton House, but the weather was fair, and after that we made good time on to Fort Pitt. We did not sleep in the open any more; we stayed inside our tents. Packs of wolves howled around us at night and followed us by day. One Friday morning, Archie shot a big wolf right near our tent.

Fort Pitt was well kept and very clean. The Hudson's Bay factor invited all the leaders of the different groups in our company to dinner, and our whole family as well, and he carved up the biggest roast I had ever seen. It was buffalo, though it tasted like juicy, rich roast beef, my favourite meat of all. Our host advised us to press on without delay. The Blackfoot and the

Cree Indians to the west were fighting each other, but he would recommend a guide who knew the trail and could help us to avoid the war parties, or negotiate with them if they confronted us: Michel, an Iroquois man.

Michel did keep us out of the way of the warring tribes. He also kept us on the trail, though it was often too faint for our scouts to see.

We had had six weeks of mainly dry weather, but that changed the day after we left Fort Pitt. Wind blew the covers off our carts, and sheets of rain soaked everything. Our way now lay through low-lying country, between hills covered with black spruce. For the next twenty days, the rain never stopped. Little streams turned into rivers. Low land turned into marsh. In three days, from July 18 to 21, our company had to build eight long bridges, sometimes over rivers, and sometimes through swampy land. Sometimes the men were able to chop down big trees and haul logs to span the streams, tying them to trees on the riverbanks. Then they placed short poles sideways on top of the long logs. There were lots of sore backs and blistered hands before anyone could cross, and more than one cart almost tipped over every time.

Swamps were even more difficult. The men waded where they could, but sometimes that was impossible. Then they had to take the wheels off the Red River carts and lay the carts end to end, upside down, to make a kind of bridge. Gus and I tried to help, but we couldn't do much. When he saw us, Papa said it was too dangerous, and we had to stay with Ma. We helped her to bake bannock for everyone.

"Maybe we should trade our carts for boats," Papa joked. "Is there anybody named Noah in this crowd?"

"Is this the over*land* trail?" Archie asked Mr. McMicking.

"It is," he replied. They were both up to their waists in water. "It is at least three feet *over* land right now." Everybody traded jokes. The wetter we got, the more we laughed. Every squelching step brought us closer to the Cariboo.

It was still raining when we came in sight of Edmonton House. As usual, we were on the wrong side of a river. At the post, men ran the Union Jack up the flagpole and fired a cannon to welcome us, but there was no way for us to cross. All the boats had been carried away in the flood, so we had to camp in the rain for four days until search parties brought them back. We cheered and fired salutes with our guns when the boats finally arrived on July 25 and ferried us over to the bustling town. We were raggedy and wet, but everyone was safe.

That Saturday, we gave a concert at our camp near Edmonton. Papa played his fiddle, Archie his tin whistle, and others performed on cornets, banjos, and horns. Two choirs sang. Mr. Morrow recited a poem about brave General Wolfe. I felt sad, thinking how he'd died on the field of battle at the Plains of Abraham, more than one hundred years ago. The French general, Montcalm, had died too.

Then Mr. Fraser, from Edmonton, marched in with his bagpipes. Four Scottish men made a cross with their Bowie knives and danced. I wanted to dance too, but Archie told me the sword dance was only for men, even if they didn't have any swords, only knives. I asked Ma to sing "Sweet Molly Malone," but she said that was enough for one night. It was the best concert of my whole life.

We spent a week in Edmonton. Papa was always busy. "We don't know which way to go," he told us. "Everybody tells a different story. We have hired a new guide: André Cardinal. I think he will be the best we have had. A good thing if he is: the worst country lies ahead."

The committee decided we should sell our carts and wagons and buy packhorses to cross the mountains. The mountains were still far away but Edmonton was the last big trading post on the way.

Papa sold the cows. Their milk had been drying up, but I missed Bossy. She never kicked any more. Papa kept one ox, Buster. I never saw an ox kick up his heels like Buster did when Papa and Alain tried to tie packs on his back. To be fair, the other oxen did not like the idea of carrying a load on their backs rather than pulling it in a cart any better than Buster; they all jumped around and bellowed. Tents, pots and pans, mining gear, and clothes were soon strewn around in the mud. Everybody knows the saying "Stubborn as an ox." I wondered then who would turn out to be more stubborn, Buster or Papa.

On August 2, we left the last tiny village before the mountains, St. Ann's. We left Mr. Morrow there as well. When he'd tried to load his ox that morning, the beast had kicked the poor man in the face. It was the same ox that had run away in the mud near Fort Ellice and dragged a cart wheel over Mr. Morrow's head.

Papa said Mr. Morrow was a slow learner. Archie laughed when I told him that.

Mr. Morrow could not go on with us, and nobody knew how long it might be before he was strong enough to climb the mountains. Archie said he'd stay, even if they both had to spend the winter in Edmonton. I felt like crying, but the rest of us couldn't wait for them.

"Cheer up," said Archie. "Mr. Morrow has a hard head; we know that already. I expect you'll see us in less than two weeks."

By then, we had been on the trail for two months.

CHAPTER N:° 8

On August 13, we saw the Rocky Mountains.
They seemed very close, but we were still one
hundred miles away. The snowy peaks hid most
of the sky. They were glorious to behold, but
there was one question I was afraid to ask. How
could we ever climb so high? At Fort Garry
I sometimes watched ants crawling. Now, when I
looked at the mountains, I felt even smaller than
an ant. Could there be a way for us to cross?

While our eyes were fixed on the great mountains, we heard shouts behind us. I turned around

and there were Archie and Mr. Morrow, riding towards us. A third horse followed them, its back piled with bundles. At last, Mr. Morrow had got rid of his ox. We were all happy to have our company together again.

On the morning of August 20, we crossed the Athabaska River. The Hudson's Bay did not keep boats there, so we had to build rafts. It made us think that maybe sixty dollars was not too much passage money after all! Alain and Pierre swam two of our horses across, leading Buster. Papa rode Star into the water, leading the packhorses. Papa asked me to look after his glasses again, and I put them in a little oilskin bag that hung around my neck.

Ma and I and the children crossed on Mr. Morrow's raft. Archie cut a sweep for me—that's a branch with little branches and leaves on the end. I picked it up and paddled like Archie and the other men, but the current tried to carry us away. Maybe it wouldn't have been so scary if we had tied the raft to two or maybe three oxen and let them help, but not if Mr. Morrow's ox had been one of them. I was glad that dangerous beast had been left behind.

We landed on a sandy beach. Mr. Wattie, one of the older men in our company, stood nearby, in water above his knees, already shaking his mining pan.

"Did you find gold?" I asked him.

"Some," he said. "Dunno how much."

"Can I try too?" I could hardly wait! "Please, Mr. Wattie?"

He laughed. "Get your pan." Then he glanced at Archie. "Have you ever washed for gold, Mr. McNaughton?"

Archie had to admit he had not.

"Well, then, how about one pan for the two of you?"

"Yes, sir!" said Archie smartly.

Ma jumped off the raft with Jamie under one arm, Mary Jane under the other, and Gus hanging on to her skirts. "Mind you take care of my big girl," Ma told Archie.

"Yes, ma'am!"

"Me too," yelled Gus.

"Me too," said Mary Jane.

Jamie would likely have said the same, except he couldn't talk much yet.

We slung our gear on shore faster than ever before. Archie got out his pan, while Ma dragged the little ones away. I could hear Gus whining, not wanting to do girls' jobs, like getting dinner and minding babies.

"Ma won't let him get away with that," I told Archie. "In our family, everyone shares the work."

"I can cook some," said Archie, "but I sure can't wash clothes. Your ma keeps all of you as smart as a new pin."

My dress was faded and my hair was coming loose. I had braided it myself, but I couldn't braid it as tight as Ma. Was Archie making fun of me? Maybe he needed glasses, like Papa. He was right about the clothes, though. Mine were clean; his shirt was grubby, and his pants were caked with mud.

"A miner has to do everything for himself," said Mr. Wattie. "I learned that in California."

I tied up my skirts and waded into the water, up to my knees. I knew I'd be walking in wet boots again that afternoon.

Mr. Wattie held out his pan. It was empty, except for a little sand in the bottom. I stirred the sand with my finger, and some tiny yellow specks gleamed in the sun.

"Is *that* all?" I was shocked.

"You expected nuggets? Everybody does. Ain't nobody gets 'em, though, except maybe one or two in a thousand. This may be the most gold we see until Cariboo. I could likely pan three, maybe four dollars a day right here. That's good money, even if it don't look like much."

"I'm sorry, Mr. Wattie."

"That's all right," he said gruffly. "You didn't know. Archie McNaughton, you're mighty quiet. Are you disappointed too?"

"I'm ignorant, James, and I've less excuse than Lisa."

"Everybody in this train is ignorant about gold," said Mr. Wattie, "except for two or three of us who've gone mining before. Some will learn, some won't. Get down there now and scoop some sand into your pan."

Archie and I were both soaking wet by the time our pan was almost half-full. I held one side and Archie held the other.

"Let the river fill 'er up," said Mr. Wattie. "Hold that pan close to the surface, like I'm doing. Shake it careful, now, to let out the sand. Gold dust is heavy; it will settle to the bottom. You'll have a sprinkle to share."

I dropped my side of the pan while he was still talking. It was too heavy. All our sand fell out.

"I should have held on tighter," said Archie, even though it was my fault.

We filled the pan again. I held my side against my knees while we rocked the pan, a little at a time, and the sand floated out like clouds into the river.

I had thought that Archie knew all about mining. Men always acted like they knew things.

Archie had strong hands, but I knew as much about panning as he did. And, thanks to Mr. Wattie, now I knew more than Papa. When we were done, I tucked a paper with a few grains of gold dust into my oilskin pouch.

The call to load up came while Archie and I were still eating our dinner. We gulped the last few mouthfuls.

"Archie," I said, "I can wash clothes. If you like, I'll wash yours."

"Can you really? Lisa, I like, believe me. I'll gladly pay you."

"I'll do it the first good day, and you don't need to pay."

The first good day would probably be Sunday, if it didn't rain. At home, Saturday night was bath night, and Monday was wash day. We kept the Sabbath holy. On the trail, however, Sunday was the only day we stopped long enough to heat water for the washtub.

"Does God mind?" I asked Ma.

Ma said cleanliness was next to godliness and

"*Gold dust is heavy; it will settle to the bottom. You'll have a sprinkle to share,*" said Mr. Wattie.

she expected God would understand.

I usually got the bath water first, after Ma. I'd wash myself all over with soap. Then, while the others took turns in the tub, I'd haul more water and set it over the fire for the laundry. Most of the men just scrubbed their clothes in a river or lake. "Too lazy to carry water and heat it," Ma would sniff. I washed the children's clothes as well as my own, to save Ma's back. I could wash Archie's clothes too.

Ma seemed to be getting fatter, but everybody else grew thinner day by day. Often, we had to lead our horses as we climbed the rocky slopes. Ma had always been sure-footed. Now, to my surprise, she sometimes crept up the steepest paths on her hands and knees. We'd left Fort Garry with supplies to last more than two months, but we had been on the trail for almost three months now and were still in the middle of the mountains. Our pemmican was almost gone.

It was a happy day when Papa brought us some

fresh meat to roast. Our guide, André Cardinal, showed us how his people do it. I helped Ma to turn the meat and move it over the fire. Oh, how good it smelled! I could hardly wait for it to be ready. And the taste! I'd never eaten anything so wonderful.

"Can we get more of that?" I asked, licking my fingers. "What kind of meat was it?"

Papa laughed. "Maybe I should not tell you."

"You can tell me. I don't care what it was." I patted my stomach.

"Skunk."

"I don't believe you."

"Skunk. And you are right, it was delicious." He collapsed in a gale of laughter. Just watching him, I started laughing too, and soon everybody joined in, holding their stomachs. We hadn't laughed like that for a long time.

"Really, *skunk*?" I still couldn't quite believe it.

Papa nodded, wiping his eyes.

Ma grinned and almost set us off again. "I've a mind to go out with a musket myself. Who knows what I might find?"

"Porcupine, maybe," said Papa. "But don't waste powder and shot on them. I can't see well enough to shoot, but even I can club a porcupine on the nose."

Turned out I was the one who found the porcupine, two days later. It stared at me with mean little eyes. Porcupines are covered with sharp quills. Other animals don't go near them. I yelled for Papa to bring his club. That meat tasted good too, though not as good as the skunk. I found huckleberries and picked enough for dinner and for supper as well. That night, we slept with full bellies.

Our mining gear was heavy, and sometimes I wondered if we would ever use it. Would we ever reach the Cariboo?

At last we had climbed to Tête Jaune Cache. If you divided our journey into three parts, we had completed two of them. But it was September 1, and our food was almost gone.

Tête Jaune—Yellowhead—was the nickname of an Iroquois trapper who used to work this area, a blond Indian, Pierre Bostonais. It was true, then: some Indians did have golden hair! I wondered if Pierre had been kidnapped, like Jamie almost was.

Now I knew why Ma was getting fatter, and why she was so tired. She was going to have another baby. I had finally asked her what was wrong, and she told me. "I'm sorry you were worried, Lisa," she added, "but let's keep this secret in the family as long as we can. Papa knows, of course, but I don't think anybody else has guessed, do you?"

I shook my head. Now I knew why Papa had wanted Ma to ride in the cart and not walk so much, and why he'd wanted her to ride on Star after we'd sold the cart. We had all been walking in the mountains, though. For two weeks, Papa, Alain, and Pierre had been carrying even more than the horses. I had my own bundle of clothes and bedding. Even Gus carried a blanket on his back.

At Tête Jaune Cache, there was feed for our animals. The horses began to get stronger. The days were warm, though the nights were cold. I wished we could stay there, but Ma fretted more every day. Winter was not far off.

Shuswap Indians lived at Tête Jaune Cache. They traded dried salmon and berry cakes. Ma traded her tea kettle.

"Papa, do you think the Shuswap will take my hair ribbons?" I asked.

"I'm sure they will. Will you trade them?"

I nodded. I loved my yellow ribbons. My father had bought them in St. Paul before he died, yellow ribbons for my golden hair. But my hair was not golden any more; the sun had turned it pale yellow, like straw. I showed one of the Shuswap squaws how to tie my ribbons. André Cardinal told her I wanted to trade.

"She will give you two big pieces of dried salmon," he told me, "and five berry cakes. I think it is a good trade."

"Thank you, André." I bowed to the Shuswap lady and took my food back to our tent.

"Well done, Lisa," said Ma. "We have you to thank for our dinner today."

"So, we are eating Lisa's hair ribbons." It was the first joke Papa had made in a long time.

"It tastes like salmon to me." I grinned back at him.

After dinner, Papa cut two leather laces for my hair. Some of the men tied their hair back with laces. Papa had started to do that, but then Ma got her scissors and cut it. Some of the other men asked her for a haircut too. They told Papa he was a lucky man, having his wife with him.

CHAPTER N.º 10

There was no one now to help us reach the Cariboo. The Indians at Tête Jaune Cache did not trade in that direction, and they knew no tribe that did. The Fraser is a fearful river, they told André Cardinal, full of rapids. The river would kill us if we went that way. Rafts would collapse, canoes would be dashed on the rocks. Horses could not possibly swim in that current.

"Is there another way?" we asked.

Our guide talked with the Shuswaps for a long time. "There is another river," he told us at last.

"It does not go to the Cariboo, but it is safer than the Fraser. We cannot stay here."

Our company had travelled together since early June. We had shared food, made music, told stories, laughed, fished and hunted, built bridges, and panned for gold. We had gone hungry, killed and eaten wild animals, sold our carts, and traded our goods. Above all, we had crossed a great country together. Nobody had died. Nobody but Mr. Morrow had been seriously hurt. Now we had to separate.

Most of the men decided to try their luck on the Fraser River. Others, including our family, agreed to take the horses and look for the Thompson River, our path to the town of Kamloops. André Cardinal said he would travel partway with us. One of the Shuswaps would also help to guide us as far as the headwaters of the river.

I remembered the long, boring meeting when this company had chosen Mr. McMicking and made all those rules. Our final meeting was short.

We dissolved the company. We wished each other godspeed. We hugged.

Archie was going on the Fraser River, along with the others from Montreal. Their rafts were loaded.

"I'll miss you," Archie told me. "You be careful, Lisa."

"You be careful too."

Most of the men wiped tears from their eyes, not just Archie and me.

CHAPTER N.°11

The first two days were easy walking on a well-marked trail. Our Shuswap guide strode ahead, and we kept up a brisk pace.

My calico dress was patched and faded. It had been tight when we'd left Fort Garry. Now it hung loose, but the sleeves were too short. For some weeks, I had worn a cloak because of the cold, but the September sun was warm. I didn't care about my old ragged dress. Maybe, I thought, we would have easy walking all the way to Kamloops.

I should have known better.

On the third day, we came to a forest. Huge fir trees grew right up to the rocky cliffs above the river. Dead giants, fallen and rotted, blocked our way. Even lying on the ground, the trunks of those trees were twice as tall as I was. There were still needles on the branches, sharp enough to draw blood. Pitch stuck to my arms.

We lost the trail, if there was any trail. Our guide could not find one. He and André Cardinal searched all day. As the shadows lengthened, we started cutting our way through the tangle. Papa would not let me take a turn with our axe. My arms were not as strong as a man's, he told me, though sometimes he used to let me split kindling.

I had to carry Jamie. Ma was carrying the new baby who was not born yet, but he or she had to be pretty big, judging from the way Ma stuck out in front. Papa took his turn with the axe, then he carried Mary Jane. We all had bundles on our backs.

I wished we could have floated down the
Fraser with Archie, instead of wading through
streams and getting cold and wet. The water was
shallow where we crossed, but Papa said the
streams would be wide and deep long before they
flowed into the ocean.

We were still in the mountains, hundreds of
miles from any ocean.

We came to a third little stream on September 7.
Our guide said he had done what he had
promised: this was the Thompson River. He
believed we could follow it to a town, although
he could not be certain, as his tribe did not
trade in that direction. We could not persuade
him to continue, so we thanked him and gave
him his pay.

"I must leave you too," said André Cardinal,
sadly. "Winter is not far off, and it's a long way
back to Edmonton."

"We'll miss you, André," said Ma.

"Me too," said Gus.

"Me too," echoed Mary Jane.

Our Shuswap guide blazed a tree, and André Cardinal carved his name, then lent me his knife to carve my name under his. Nobody had much to say when we stopped to eat that day. I'm sure we all missed André's confidence and skill, as well as his cheerful laughter.

For the first few days after we left Tête Jaune Cache, Mary Jane cried and cried. I got tired of asking her what was wrong. "Me hungry," she said, or "Me tired." I carried a piece of bannock and gave her little bits, but there wasn't much, and it didn't keep her quiet for long. Then she stopped crying. Her face got a pinched look. Papa picked her up when he could. Pierre took Gus by the hand. Alain carried Jamie when I stumbled. There must have been at least one Sabbath, likely two, but we did not stop to pray or rest. We did not care what day it was. We were all bone-weary.

Papa was right; soon the river grew wide enough for rafts and canoes. Then we came up against a wall of rock. The river tumbled through a gorge, far below.

"I give up," said Papa in disgust. "This is for mountain goats, not for people. I vote we stop and build some rafts."

There was another reason we had to stop. We had eaten all our food. It was time to kill some oxen and dry the meat over the fire.

"Hurry up," said Ma.

There were plenty of trees to make rafts, but Papa worried about Ma. "You'll be wet and cold, Catherine," he fretted. "I'd like to make a canoe."

Ma shook her head. "No time," she said. "Lisa, take Gus and go after firewood. See if you can haul in a dead tree."

We kept the fire going for three days to dry our beef. September 21 was the Sabbath. We worked all day, pausing only to say special prayers after dinner.

"We are lost in the wilderness," said Papa. "Guide us to a safe place, Lord."

"Are you scared because we're lost?" I asked him.

Papa thought for a moment. "We have food, we

are together, and this river will carry us," he said at last. "Maybe I should be scared, but right now I'm not."

"Then I'm not scared either," I told him.

Monday was sunny, but a cold wind blew through our clothes. Papa spread oiled cloth on our raft and used it to bundle up Ma and the little ones. The raft looked big, but it was crowded with five men, three horses, and piles of baggage, as well as the lumpy bundle in the middle, with Ma's head sticking out. I took a pole, like the men. The water was shallow. Our raft kept getting caught on dead trees.

We travelled this way for two days; then the river deepened. At last we were gliding along. Papa kept three people at the front of our raft to watch for dead trees or rocks. I kneeled in the middle and hung on. The days were shorter now, but we found plenty of flat places where we could steer our rafts ashore and set up a rough camp.

On Saturday morning, two rafts left before we

did. We swung around a bend in the river and saw them—beached.

"Rapids!" the men shouted.

Our raft shot forward in the current. Our poles dug in frantically, driving us towards the shore and safety.

"Jump, men," Papa yelled. "Help me hold her."

Then everything happened in a sort of blur. I saw Papa in water above his waist. More men splashed in after him. Baggage tumbled. The horses bucked and tried to break loose. Ma's mouth was open, but I couldn't hear her. I ran to untie the oiled cloth. Ma jumped, with Jamie under one arm and Mary Jane under the other, just as the current caught the raft and tore it loose. I saw the horror on Papa's face as the river whirled the rest of us out of sight.

Somebody screamed louder than the horses. Perhaps it was me, perhaps one of the men. Gus still huddled in the dark cloth. I remember thinking he was too close to the horses, he'd be hurt if one of them got loose. Somehow I got him away.

Our raft raced towards white water that foamed and roared around sharp rocks. One dark, jagged point rose straight in front of us. I grabbed Gus and threw myself down, just as we struck.

Next I remember, I was on the huge rock. My right arm pressed Gus to my body; my left arm braced us against the stone. Tears filled my eyes— for the horses, poor beasts, more than for Gus or me. I was not thinking, it was just a feeling: horses, and sadness, and tears.

My feet were on a ledge, not quite in the river, but cold spray beat against Gus and me as it roared by. I faced upstream, the way we had come, but could not see Papa or anybody else. I did not dare turn my head to see if anyone else had been saved. I shivered, and wondered if I would ever stop.

My left hand went numb. Slowly, I let go of the rock and changed arms. For a moment, my legs and back held us, nothing else. Then my right hand, warmed by Gus's body, found the rock. I stamped my feet, carefully. I changed arms again, and again.

*"Hang on, girlie,
I'm coming."*

At last there was a shout from shore: "Hang on, girlie, I'm coming."

Then a dugout canoe raced towards us, steered by a big man, a trapper. I knew him, but I couldn't think of his name.

How could any human being rescue us? How could a man hold his craft steady without being torn away from our rock, or dashed to pieces against it? It should have been impossible, but it was not. One huge hand reached for Gus. My arm seemed frozen around his little body, but then I managed to let go. Our rescuer lifted Gus into the canoe, then me.

"Keep down," he grunted. Then he threw all his strength into paddling to shore.

Two more men still clung to a higher part of that rock. I hadn't known anyone else was there. The dugout canoe had to make two more trips before all four of us were safe.

I have seen Papa hug another man, but not often, and never like he did that day. The big trapper hugged him back. His name was Andrew Holes.

The next afternoon we found two of the horses on the riverbank. They were bruised and cut, but alive! I would not have believed it if I had not seen it for myself. We never saw the other horse again.

Our prayers on that Sabbath were brief, but from our hearts.

The rapids were called Porte d'Enfer, which means Hell's Gate. There was another Hell's Gate on the Fraser River, but Porte d'Enfer was longer and more dangerous. Altogether, our party lost four rafts and three canoes. One man drowned when he panicked and tried to swim to shore. I am glad I did not see it happen.

The rapids were nine miles long. We had to carry everything that we had saved over those nine miles. The parcel with our precious papers was part of my load. Rain and even wet snow made walking a miscry, but I was glad of every step, glad that I was alive to take it.

A few short weeks before, I had thought I would never be happy until I reached the Cariboo. Now, I did not care. Finding gold did not matter any more.

Before the end of that nine miles, we met four miners going the other way. At last we knew where we were, two hundred miles from Fort Kamloops.

"Watch out for more rapids," the miners told us, "but there's only one more bad place. You can walk from there. You'll see another river flowing into this one. Look to your left; you can't miss the Kamloops trail."

Below Hell's Gate, we built more rafts, though not so many now, as so much baggage had been lost. After two easy days on the river, we heard the roar of rapids again. Nobody tried to run them. We had learned our lesson. We abandoned our rafts and carried our goods along the river-bank until we found a good campsite.

After supper, Andrew Holes came to visit. Ma was wearing a dress like a tent. He looked at her, then looked down at the ground. His face turned red.

"Most everybody is taking the trail to Kamloops," he said at last. "I guess you'll be wanting to build another raft. I'll stay and help, and travel with you, if you'll have me."

Ma could not find her voice. I could.

"That's very kind of you, Mr. Holes," I said, like Ma would have done. "We would be glad to have you."

"It would be an honour," Papa added.

Ma laughed. "A raft sounds mighty fine to me," she said. "I did not relish the notion of walking another hundred miles."

CHAPTER N°12

The four men built a fine big raft, with a railing and flat stones for a hearth. That was Mr. Holes's idea. "If we can cook our food on the raft," he said, "we won't have to stop for dinner."

I carried water and made fires and cooked and washed and sang the little ones to sleep. Ma helped a good bit, but she moved slowly and tired fast.

When we set off once more, Ma had the black oiled cloth around her, but this time it was not tied. We would not make that mistake again.

When the sun went down, the men looked for a place to camp. "Don't stop," Ma urged.

"It's too dangerous," said Papa. "Rocks, snags, rapids—anything could happen in the dark."

"Are you going to wait until our food is gone? Until there is snow on the ground? Until..." Ma looked down and patted her big belly. She would not talk about the baby and how soon it might be born.

"The moon is full," said Mr. Holes. "I'll take the sweep to start with. Let's go on."

The moon rose ahead of us, a giant golden plate. It threw a band of pale gold over the river. Water gently slapped against the timbers of our raft. I lay awake but dreamy, warm under a buffalo robe, snuggled between Papa and Gus. Mr. Holes held the long pole, but the river carried us peacefully, and we struck no snags.

For two more days and nights we floated slowly down the river. Snags and rocks were few, and easy enough to avoid. We ate the last of our dried meat. There was enough flour to make bannock for one more day.

We had to tie up, so that Pierre, Alain, and Mr. Holes could go hunting. Papa and I searched for cranberries, the only berry we could expect to find so late in the year. The hunters brought back three squirrels and two pigeons. With these, berries, and bannock, Ma and I prepared a fine supper. Afterwards, the men cleaned their muskets. Papa gave his ammunition to Mr. Holes, and so did Pierre and Alain.

"You are the best marksman," Papa said. "We must not waste a single shot."

Mr. Holes hunted while our raft floated on. "I can make good time following the riverbank," he said. He brought meat for two more days, but that was the end of the gunpowder.

All of us were used to going hungry, but we were not used to starvation. I could not stop thinking about food. If I dozed off, I dreamed of sinking my teeth into juicy meat. My stomach churned. I drank water and more water, but it did not help. Gus and Mary Jane whined. Jamie whimpered. He did not rouse much even when

Ma sang "London Bridge is falling down" and his other favourite songs.

The next day, it was hard to get up at all.

"Rock ahead," called Mr. Holes. I held my sweep over the side, but I could not hang on to it, let alone help steer the raft. All the men moved slowly. We missed the rock, but not by much.

Nobody said anything, but we knew we had to find food, or we would die. The day was gloomy, and I almost missed the sight that saved us: tipis. I blinked, and the village was still there, hidden in the trees. "Stop!" I intended to yell, but my voice was more of a croak. The men heard me, however, and soon we were ashore, Ma and everyone.

No Indians came out to greet us. No smoke rose from the tents. Perhaps everybody was gone. Then we came to the potato patch. One and all, we fell to our knees and scrabbled in the rich dirt, clawing up the potatoes. We ate them raw, dirt and all. Ma and I filled our aprons.

Jamie wandered off towards the nearest tipi,

and Pierre went after him. They came back in an instant.

"Smallpox," Pierre said, trembling. "They're all dead."

Weak as we were, we ran. We kept our potatoes, though, and cooked a feast of them. That dead village saved our lives.

The next day, we ate potatoes again, and nibbled on rosehips that we found along the shore.

Then our food was gone once more. Again, we saw tipis, and smoke rising in little puffs. Food! All of us rushed towards the village, except for Ma and Gus, who stayed on the raft. "Hurry back," Ma told us. "This baby could be born any time."

It was the first time she had talked about the baby in front of the men, but nobody seemed surprised. "We'll hurry," Papa promised.

Maybe I should have stayed on the raft. None of us could talk the Shuswap language, though, so it likely didn't make any difference. People can rub their bellies to show they are hungry, and they can hold out things they have, and point to things they want. People can trade, even if they cannot talk. We had only gained a few potatoes and one scrawny rabbit, though, when Gus came running for help.

I've laughed lots of times since, thinking about it, but nobody laughed that day. Back at the raft, an old Indian woman was busy untying the black cowhide rope. In another moment, Ma would have floated away. The old woman and Ma were yelling at each other, both red-faced and furious. As we came up, Ma caught up a piece of firewood, ready to smash it down on the old woman's fingers.

What was the matter? We had no way of telling. Sign language was no use. The other Indians now looked angry as well. We jumped aboard and pushed off. We got to know those

Indians later, at Kamloops. The old woman had lost a black cow, only a day or two before we came to their village. She was sure we had stolen her cow and made the rope out of its hide. Too bad we could not talk to her at the time.

CHAPTER № 13

There was a story that Indian women helped Ma when the baby was born and wanted her to name the baby Kamloops, because that's where she was born. The Indian women did help, but that was later. We had not reached Kamloops when the baby was ready to be born. I was there. I know.

When Ma said we had to stop, the men put up a tent. Papa and I tended her, nobody else. The other men made a fire and heated some water. We didn't have a cooking pot any more, only a

*"We have a fine daughter,
my love."*

tin cup, but it helped. Papa held the baby, and I washed her off the best I could.

"She's not much bigger than a doll." I was worried. Ma's stomach had stuck out a mile, but our baby was so small. Suddenly she yawned. Her mouth stretched wide open, then shut again, as if she had surprised herself. Oh, I loved her, I felt warm all over with love.

"She's about the same size as the others," said Papa. "'Bout the same size as you were, I expect. Don't you worry, Lisa, she'll grow." He turned to Ma. "We have a fine little daughter, my love."

Ma held out her arms to hold the baby, though it was easy to see she was very tired. "You helped, Lisa," she said softly. "You should choose her name."

It took me a day or two, but I named her Rose, for the rosehips we ate, and for her red cheeks, and because it was pretty, and Rose was the prettiest baby ever.

Not many girls get to help when a baby is born. Not many men either, said Papa, and he'd rather not have to again. I felt different from him, though. It was scary, sure, but it was amazing too. Hearing her first cry, little baby Rose, that was more of a thrill, way more, than finding those tiny specks of gold in the bottom of my pan. Maybe I won't be a miner, I thought. Maybe I could be a midwife, and help lots of women when their babies are born.

Little Rose spent her first winter in Kamloops. Archie had said he would write to me there. "Remember," he reminded me, "a McNaughton never goes back on his word."

Nobody ever wrote a letter to me yet. I get excited just thinking about it. Maybe, in the spring, we'll go to Cariboo.

ACKNOWLEDGEMENTS

THIS STORY HAS FASCINATED ME FOR MORE THAN THIRTY YEARS.
In addition to Margaret McNaughton's original book, enriched by
storytellers in my family, I acknowledge with appreciation the
work of many others. Victor Hopwood edited the 1973 edition of
McNaughton's work, with a most useful introduction; he also
inspired his university colleagues to edit other primary sources,
notably Joanne Leduc, editor of Thomas McMicking's articles,
published in book form in 1981. Internet searches turned up other
material, especially from the B.C. archives. Agnes Laut's 1916
chronicle is not always reliable, but she talked to some of the old-
timers and provides some wonderful details. Other secondary
sources include Mark Wade, Vicky Metcalf, and W. Kaye Lamb.
Richard Thomas Wright's *Overlanders*, 1985, is much the most useful
recent book, including maps and lists of people and equipment.
Wright comments that Native and Metis women regularly travelled
with their menfolk, notwithstanding pregnancy; he downplays
Catherine Schubert's fortitude. No woman who has experienced
pregnancy and given birth would do so.

Dear Reader,

Did you enjoy reading this Our Canadian Girl adventure? Write us and tell us what you think! We'd love to hear about your favourite parts, which characters you like best, and even whom else you'd like to see stories about. Maybe you'd like to read an adventure with one of Our Canadian Girls that happened in your home-town—fifty, a hundred years ago or more!

Send your letters to:

> Our Canadian Girl
> c/o Penguin Canada
> 10 Alcorn Avenue, Suite 300
> Toronto, ON M4V 3B2

Be sure to check your bookstore for more books in the Our Canadian Girl series. There are some ready for you right now, and more are on their way.

We look forward to hearing from you!

Sincerely,

> *Barbara Berson*
> PENGUIN CANADA

P.S. *Don't forget to visit us online at www.ourcanadiangirl.ca—there are some other girls you should meet!*

Canada's

1608
Samuel de Champlain establishes the first fortified trading post at Quebec.

1759
The British defeat the French in the Battle of the Plains of Abraham.

1812
The United States declares war against Canada.

1845
The expedition of Sir John Franklin to the Arctic ends when the ship is frozen in the pack ice; the fate of its crew remains a mystery.

1869
Louis Riel leads his Metis followers in the Red River Rebellion.

1871
British Columbia joins Canada.

1755
The British expel the entire French population of Acadia (today's Maritime provinces), sending them into exile.

1776
The 13 Colonies revolt against Britain, and the Loyalists flee to Canada.

1837
Calling for responsible government, the Patriotes, following Louis-Joseph Papineau, rebel in Lower Canada; William Lyon Mackenzie leads the uprising in Upper Canada.

1867
New Brunswick, Nova Scotia and the United Province of Canada come together in Confederation to form the Dominion of Canada.

1870
Manitoba joins Canada. The Northwest Territories become an official territory of Canada.

1784
Rachel

1862
Lisa

Timeline

1885
At Craigellachie, British Columbia, the last spike is driven to complete the building of the Canadian Pacific Railway.

1898
The Yukon Territory becomes an official territory of Canada.

1914
Britain declares war on Germany, and Canada, because of its ties to Britain, is at war too.

1918
As a result of the Wartime Elections Act, the women of Canada are given the right to vote in federal elections.

1945
World War II ends conclusively with the dropping of atomic bombs on Hiroshima and Nagasaki.

1873
Prince Edward Island joins Canada.

1896
Gold is discovered on Bonanza Creek, a tributary of the Klondike River.

1905
Alberta and Saskatchewan join Canada.

1917
In the Halifax harbour, two ships collide, causing an explosion that leaves more than 1,600 dead and 9,000 injured.

1939
Canada declares war on Germany seven days after war is declared by Britain and France.

1949
Newfoundland, under the leadership of Joey Smallwood, joins Canada.

1896
Emily

1885
Marie-Claire

1944
Margit

Check out the
Our Canadian Girl website

Fun Stuff

- E-cards
- Prizes
- Activities
- Polls

Fan Area

- Guest Book
- Photo Gallery
- Downloadable *Our Canadian Girl* Tea Party Kit

Features on the girls and more!

www.ourcanadiangirl.ca